No Babysitters Allowed

No Babysit

Amber Stewart

ters Allowed

illustrated by Laura Rankin

BLOOMSBURY
CHILDREN'S
BOOKS

First published in Great Britain in 2009 by Bloomsbury Publishing Plc
36 Soho Square, London, W1D 3QY

First published in the USA in 2008 by Bloomsbury USA Children's Books
175 Fifth Avenue, New York, NY 10010

Text copyright © by Amber Stewart 2008
Illustrations copyright © by Laura Rankin 2008
The moral rights of the author and illustrator have been asserted

A CIP catalogue record of this book is available from the British Library

ISBN 978 0 7475 9847 3

Printed in China by South China Printing Co

1 3 5 7 9 10 8 6 4 2

Mixed Sources
Product group from well-managed
forests, and other controlled sources
www.fsc.org Cert no. SCS-COC-00927
© 1996 Forest Stewardship Council
FSC

www.bloomsbury.com/childrens

For my mum
— A. S.

In loving memory of my mother,
Mary Rankin
— L. R.

Hopscotch was Mummy's brave boy.

He was so brave he could take a spider that came visiting
back out into the garden, when Mummy wasn't sure,

and when he fell off his tricycle and had to have a
sticky plaster on his leg, he didn't cry at all.

There were many things that Hopscotch could do
very, very bravely.

But when Hopscotch realised that tonight was a
Mrs Honeybunch-the-babysitter night,

he didn't feel brave at all.

'Sweetheart,' Mummy said,
'don't you like Mrs Honeybunch?'
'No,' said Hopscotch. 'Rabbity and
I do not like Mrs Honeybunch.'

But really, Hopscotch didn't like bedtime without
Mummy and Daddy. It made him feel all worried inside,
and that made his tummy hurt.

'I have a hurt tummy, Mummy,' Hopscotch said hopefully. 'You can't go out when my tummy is worried.'

'Mrs Honeybunch can give you warm milk for that,' smiled Daddy, kissing him better. 'Rabbity can have some too.'

'Just go, we'll be fine,' said Mrs Honeybunch
kindly.
Mummy was looking as worried as Hopscotch.

Hopscotch and Rabbity pressed their noses to the goodbye window, still waving long after Mummy and Daddy had turned the corner out of sight.

'Now, Hopscotch,' smiled Mrs Honeybunch, 'what shall
we do? Shall we paint a picture?'

Hopscotch and Rabbity just pressed their noses closer
to the goodbye window and gave a little sniff.

'What about building a car
from your blocks?' suggested
Mrs Honeybunch.
   They gave a slightly bigger sniff.

'I know!' said Mrs Honeybunch
brightly. 'Let's play hide-and-seek.'
   Hopscotch shook his head sadly.
'No, thank you,' he sighed. 'I think
I will play hiding and no seeking
all by myself.'

And off Hopscotch went to hide in the special
No Babysitters Allowed camp that he had made.
He even put Rabbity outside to guard the entrance.

Hiding is fun when someone is seeking, but hiding on your own when no one is looking for you is very boring,

as Hopscotch soon discovered.

There was not much to do in his camp, especially with Rabbity on guard duty.

It might have been fun to build a car, or paint a picture . . .

So, when he heard Mrs Honeybunch ask if Rabbity
would like to hear a story while he guarded the entrance,
Hopscotch pricked up his ears, particularly as it was one
of his favourite bedtime stories.

But then the oddest thing happened. Mrs Honeybunch got the story all muddled up. She started in the middle, made up all the names and then made up the story altogether. And she did this with not one book, not two, but *three*, until Hopscotch could stand it no longer . . .

...and burst out of his camp.

'Mrs Honeybunch,' he said, 'you are reading the stories
all wrong. You are all in a muddle.'

'Oh dear, sweetheart, am I?' Mrs Honeybunch smiled.
'Perhaps you could help me out of the muddle.'

So Hopscotch very patiently told Mrs Honeybunch
all about the stories in the books …

. . . and then showed her how to
build a racing car from bricks and,
last of all, how to paint a picture
of a lovely sunny day.

Then Mrs Honeybunch
showed Hopscotch how to
make delicious warm milk
and tucked him into bed.

Much later that evening, Mummy tiptoed into his bedroom to give him a kiss goodnight.

'How is your tummy, poppet?' she asked.
'My tummy is not worried any more,' whispered Hopscotch
sleepily. 'Mrs Honeybunch can come and play again.'